THE ULTIMATE BOOK OF FOOTBALL JOKES

ILLUSTRATED BY
SADIE GARDNER

THE ULTIMATE
PLAYER JOKES
3-14

THE ULTIMATE
CLUB JOKES
16-21

THE ULTIMATE
FOOTBALL JOKES
23-52

THE ULTIMATE FOOTY
KNOCK-KNOCK JOKES
54-59

THE ULTIMATE HILARIOUS
FOOTY QUOTES
61-76

THE ULTIMATE
FOOTBALL FACTS
78-100

THE ULTIMATE
PLAYER JOKES

WHERE DO PREMIER LEAGUE FOOTBALL PLAYERS EAT THEIR DINNER?

On the premier league table!

HOW DOES THE BRIGHTON & HOVE ALBION DEFENDER LIKE HIS BISCUITS WITH HIS TEA?

He liked to Dunk them in!

WHAT DOES CRISTIANO RONALDO AND MAGICIANS HAVE IN COMMON?

They both do hat-tricks!

WHAT DO YOU CALL A FAULTY COMPUTER THAT CAN'T SAVE ANYTHING?

Kepa Arrizabalaga

WHY DO NEYMAR AND SALAH LIKE SWIMMING SO MUCH?

Because they both love diving!

WHY DID THE BARCELONA CAPTAIN HAVE TO HIRE A CLEANER?

Because he was very Messi!

WHO IS THE MOST GREEDIEST FOOTBALL MANAGER?

Jose MORE-inho!

WHAT DID SOLSKJAER SAY TO HIS PLAYER THAT HAD BEEN PLAYING BADLY?

"I am Gunnar have to sell you."

WHAT DO YOU DO WHEN YOU'RE IN LIVERPOOL AND SOMEONE STEALS YOUR CAR?

You call the Klopps!

WHY DOES IT SEEM LIKE JOSE MOURINHO HAD HURT HIS LEG AT TOTTENHAM HOTSPUR?

He relies too much on a Kane!

WHAT DO YOU CALL A FRENCH FOOTBALLER PLAYING A NINTENDO CONSOLE?

Thierry on Wii.

WHAT IS THE BEST CURRENCY TO USE IF YOU SUPPORT MANCHESTER CITY?

Raheem Sterling

IF YOU OFFER BRUNO FERNANDES A TEA AND HE DOESN'T WANT ONE, WHAT DOES HE SAY?

Brew? No.

HOW DOES THE MANCHESTER CITY BOSS PROTECT HIS HOUSE AT NIGHT?

He uses a Guardiola!

WHAT IS HEUNG-MIN SON'S FATHER CALLED?

Heung-min Dad!

WHAT IS MANCHESTER UNITED'S GOALKEEPER REALLY GOOD AT?

He's really good in De Gea.

WHY COULDN'T MANCHESTER UNITED FIND A REPLACEMENT FOR THEIR LEFT BACK?

They couldn't be too Shaw!

WHICH FOOTBALLER SLIPS THE MOST WHEN PLAYING FOOTBALL?

Antonio GREASE-man!

WHO WAS THE HORSE'S FAVOURITE FOOTBALLER?

NEIGH-mar!

WHAT IS MOHAMMED SALAH'S FAVOURITE FOOD?

Fruit Salah!

WHO WAS THE SHEEP'S FAVOURITE FOOTBALLER?

Paul PogBAAAAA!

WHICH FOOTBALLER MAKES THE BEST COFFEE?

Diego Costa!

WHAT DO YOU CALL SOMEONE WHO LOOKS UP TO NEYMAR'S DIVING?

A roll model!

HOW DOES NEYMAR LAUGH?

"ROFL"

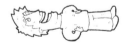

THE ULTIMATE
CLUB JOKES

WHY DID THE CHAMPIONS LEAGUE TROPHY RUN AWAY?

Because it grew two legs!

WHAT DO YOU CALL A CLUB THAT COPIES REAL MADRID?

Fake Madrid.

WHAT ARE ASTON VILLA FAN'S FAVOURITE FLAVOUR OF ICE CREAM?

Aston Vanilla!

WHAT'S THE DIFFERENCE BETWEEN TOTTENHAM HOTSPUR AND A TEABAG?

The teabags stay in the cup!

WHAT TEAM DO BUILDERS SUPPORT THE MOST?

The Hammers!

WHY DO KIDS LOVE WEST HAM UNITED SO MUCH?

Because they'll be blowing bubbles!

WHAT IS AN EVERTON FAN'S FAVOURITE SWEET TREAT?

The toffees!

WHAT IS THE DIFFERENCE BETWEEN A LIVERPOOL SUPPORTER AND A BABY

The baby will stop whining after awhile.

WHAT IS AN ELDERLY PERSON'S FAVOURITE FOOTBALL STADIUM?

Old Trafford!

IF BARCELONA VS REAL MADRID IS 'EL CLASICO', WHAT IS MANCHESTER CITY VS PSG?

El Cashico!

WHAT IS A SHEEP'S FAVOURITE TEAM?

Baaaaaaaa-celona!

WHAT DO CHELSEA AND THE US NAVY HAVE IN COMMON?

They both spent 50 million on a sub!

THE ULTIMATE
FOOTBALL
JOKES

WHY DO FOOTBALL PLAYERS LOVE THE FILM 'CINDERELLA' SO MUCH?

Because she goes to the ball!

WHY DIDN'T THE CHICKEN CROSS THE FOOTBALL PITCH?

Because it would be offside!

WHAT FOOD DID THE PLAYERS GET TO CELEBRATE WINNING THE QUARTER-FINALS?

Quarter pounder with cheese!

WHY DID THE TEAM OF 15-YEAR-OLDS GET KNOCKED OUT OF THE COMPETITION?

Because they couldn't reach the round of 16!

WHAT DID THE JUDGE DO TO THE FOOTBALL PLAYER AFTER HE WAS FOUND GUILTY OF STEALING?

He gave him a red card!

WHERE IS THE BEST PLACE IN AMERICA TO FIND A FOOTBALL KIT?

New Jersey!

WHY ARE FOOTBALL PLAYERS SO COOL IN THE HOT WEATHER?

Because they have a lot of fans!

WHAT IS A GOALKEEPERS FAVOURITE SNACK?

Beans on post!

WHY DID BOTH FOOTBALL TEAMS TURN UP WITH CUTLERY FOR THE MATCH?

Because both teams wanted a draw!

WHY DON'T GRASSHOPPERS LIKE FOOTBALL?

They prefer cricket!

WHAT DID THE MANAGER DO WHEN THE PITCH FLOODED?

He sent on all his subs!

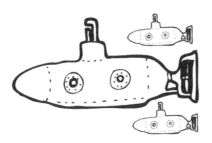

WHAT DID THE REFEREE SAY TO THE SOUTH AMERICAN AFTER HE LIED ABOUT HANDLING THE BALL?

I don't Bolivia!

WHY DID THE FOOTBALL LEAVE THE GAME?

It was tired of getting kicked around!

WHY WAS THE FOOTBALL SO ANGRY WHEN LEAVING THE STADIUM?

Because he got kicked out!

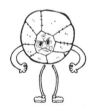

WHAT TEA DO FOOTBALLERS DRINK?

Penal-tea!

WHAT DO FOOTBALLERS DO ON OPPOSITE DAY WHEN THEY START A GAME?

They kick-on!

WHAT DO BABIES AND FOOTBALLERS HAVE IN COMMON?

They both like to dribble!

WHY DID THE PLAYER COME ON TO THE PITCH WITH A PIECE OF ROPE?

Because he was the skipper!

WHY DON'T THEY HAVE FOOTBALL STADIUMS IN MARS?

Because there is no atmosphere!

WHAT'S THE BEST POSITION FOR SOMEBODY WHO IS NOT GOOD AT FOOTBALL?

Right back…. Right back to the changing rooms.

WHAT DO YOU HAVE TO DO IF YOU ARE ADDICTED TO FOOTBALL?

You have to kick the habit!

WHY DID THE GREEDY FOOTBALLER DO SO BAD AT HIS SCHOOL EXAMS?

Because he couldn't pass!

WHAT DO YOU CALL A BOAT FULL OF POLITE AND HONEST FOOTBALLERS?

A good sportsman ship!

WHAT DO YOU CALL A GOALKEEPER THAT CAN RAP?

Posts Malone

HOW DO YOU LIGHT UP A FOOTBALL STADIUM AT NIGHT?

With a football match!

WHY DON'T FISH PLAY FOOTBALL?

They are terrified of nets!

DID YOU HEAR ABOUT THE FOOTBALL PITCH THEY BUILT ON THE MOON?

They used astroturf!

WHY SHOULD YOU NOT BREAK UP WITH YOUR PARTNER IF THEY PLAY IN GOAL?

Because they are keepers!

WHY COULDN'T THE CAR PLAY FOOTBALL?

Because it only had one boot!

WHAT DID THE COMMENTATOR SAY WHEN ALL THE ANIMALS RAN INTO THE STADIUM?

"And the crowd goes wild!!!"

WHAT WOULD YOU CALL FOOTBALL IF YOU WEREN'T ALLOWED TO WEAR ANY FOOTBALL BOOTS?

Socker!

ARE LIGHTNING BOLTS GOOD AT FOOTBALL?

No, they're shocking!

WHAT PLAYER OF THE FOOTBALL TEAM DRIVES A SHIP?

The captain!

WHAT DO YOU CALL A CRAZY BRAZILIAN FAN?

A Brazil nut!

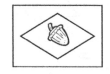

REFEREE: "I'M SENDING YOU OFF!"
PLAYER: "WHAT FOR!?"
REFEREE: "FOR THE REST OF THE MATCH, DUMMY!"

WHY AREN'T CLOWNS INCLUDED IN A FOOTBALLER'S DIET?

Because they taste funny!

WHY DON'T TEACHERS MAKE GOOD FOOTBALLERS?

Because they always lose their markers!

WHAT DO YOU HEAR ABOUT THE 100 YEAR OLD FOOTBALL PLAYER?

He's still alive and kicking!

WHICH FOOTBALLER IS IN CHARGE OF KEEPING THE FIELD NEAT?

The sweeper.

WHY ISN'T THE WORLD CUP EVER HELD IN THE JUNGLE?

There would be too many cheetahs!

WHAT DO YOU CALL A DINOSAUR WHO PLAYS AS A STRIKER?

A dino-score!

WHY DID THE DOG NOT WANT TO PLAY FOOTBALL?

Because the dog was a boxer!

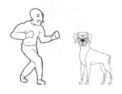

WHAT DID THE BUMBLE BEE SAY WHEN HE SCORED A GOAL?

Hive scored!

HOW DO HENS ENCOURAGE THEIR FAVOURITE FOOTBALL TEAMS?

They egg them on!

WHY COULDN'T THE SKELETON PLAY FOOTBALL?

He had no body to play with!

WHEN IS A FOOTBALL PLAYER LIKE A JUDGE?

When he sits on the bench.

WHY DO PEOPLE BECOME PROFESSIONAL FOOTBALLERS?

Because they get a kick out of it!

WHAT DOES A FOOTBALL PLAYER SAY ON HALLOWEEN?

"Hat Trick or Treat!"

WHY DID THE FOOTBALL SAY "OUCH!"

Because someone kicked it!

WHY CAN'T YOU PLAY FOOTBALL WITH PIGS?

They always hog the ball!

WHY ARE FOOTBALLERS SO ARTISTIC?

Because most games end with a draw.

WHY DID THE GOALKEEPER SAY TO THE BALL AT THE END OF THE GAME?

"Catch ya later!"

WHAT DID THE NAUGHTY FOOTBALL COMMENTATOR GET FOR CHRISTMAS?

COOOOOOOOALLL!

WHY DO GOALKEEPERS SPEND SO MUCH TIME ON THE COMPUTER?

Because they need to save all of their work!

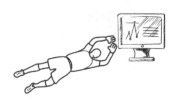

WHY DID THE FOOTBALLER HOLD HIS BOOT TO HIS EAR?

Because he enjoyed sole music!

WHY WASN'T THE NOSE IN THE MATCH DAY SQUAD?

It didn't get picked!

HOW DO YOU STOP SQUIRRELS PLAYING FOOTBALL IN THE GARDEN?

Hide the ball, it drives them nuts!

WHY IS FOOTBALL SUCH A STRANGE GAME?

Because people are running away from their goals.

WHERE DO FOOTBALLERS GO TO DANCE?

To the foot-ball!

WHY DID THE STRIKER GO TO JAIL?

Because he shot the ball!

THE ULTIMATE
KNOCK, KNOCK
JOKES

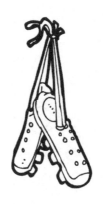

KNOCK KNOCK
Who's there?

ANNETTE.
Annette who?

ANNETTE NEEDS TO GO BETWEEN
THOSE GOALPOSTS

KNOCK KNOCK
Who's there?

HITZ CUMMINGS.
Hitz Cummings who?

HITZ CUMMING HOME, HITZ
CUMMING HOME, HITZ CUMMINGS,
FOOTBALL'S COMING HOME!

KNOCK KNOCK
Who's there?

LES
Les who?

LES GO TO A FOOTBALL MATCH!

KNOCK KNOCK
Who's there?

MAN U.
Man U Who?

MAN, U REALLY NEED TO GET A LIFE!

KNOCK KNOCK
Who's there?

HARRY.
Harry who?

HARRY UP AND SCORE, HARRY KANE, WERE DOWN 3-1!

KNOCK KNOCK
Who's there?

DOZEN.
Dozen Who?

DOZEN ANYBODY KNOW WHEN TOTTENHAM WILL WIN A TROPHY?

KNOCK KNOCK
Who's there?

SOCCER.
Soccer who?

SOCC-SER IN THE DRAWER!

KNOCK KNOCK
Who's there?

URIAH.
Uriah Who?

KEEP URAIH ON THE BALL!

KNOCK KNOCK
Who's there?

WANDA.
Wanda who?

WANDA BUY A NEW FOOTBALLL?

KNOCK KNOCK
Who's there?

ANITA
Anita Who?

ANITA MAKE A SUBSTITUTION!

KNOCK KNOCK
Who's there?

OWEN.
Owen who?

OWEN 3-0!

KNOCK KNOCK
Who's there?

MESSI.
Messi Who?

MESSI IN HERE, BETTER GIVE IT A CLEAN!

THE ULTIMATE
HILARIOUS
FOOTBALL
QUOTES

"THAT WOULD'VE BEEN A GOAL HAD IT GONE INSIDE THE POST."

Michael owen

"I DON'T HAVE ANY TATTOOS, BUT THAT'S MAINLY BECAUSE NONE OF MY LIMBS ARE WIDE ENOUGH TO SUPPORT A VISIBLE IMAGE."

Peter Crouch

"I THOUGHT WE PLAYED QUITE WELL ACTUALLY."

Sir Alex Ferguson after losing 5-0 to Newcaslte United.

"...THAT'S HIS JOB."

Roy Keane

"INZAGHI WAS BORN OFFSIDE."

Sir Alex Ferguson

"WHEN THEY DON'T SCORE, THEY HARDLY EVER WIN."

Michael Owen

"FOOTBALL IS A SIMPLE GAME; 22 MEN CHASE A BALL FOR 90 MINUTES AND AT THE END, THE GERMANS WIN."

Gary Linekar

"THEY DIDN'T GET ANGRY BECAUSE I TOOK MY SHIRT OFF AND GOT BOOKED, THEY SAW MY PHYSIQUE AND GOT JEALOUS."

Mario Balotelli

"I TRIED TO WATCH THE TOTTENHAM MATCH ON TELEVISION IN MY HOTEL, BUT I FELL ASLEEP."

Arsene Wenger

"WHAT A NIGHT! YOU NEED A HATTRICK? CALL ME!"

Erling Haaland

"ZLATAN DOESN'T DO AUDITIONS."

Zlatan Ibrahimovic when offered a trial at Arsenal.

"I CAN'T HELP BUT LAUGH AT HOW PERFECT I AM."

Zlatan Ibrahimovic

"WHEN YOU ARE 4-0 UP YOU SHOULD NEVER LOSE 7-1."

Lawrie McMenemy

"I WOULD NOT BE BOTHERED IF WE LOST EVERY GAME AS LONG AS WE WON THE LEAGUE."

Mark Viduka

"GOOD EBENING."

Unai Emery

"PLEASE DON'T CALL ME ARROGANT,
BUT I AM A EUROPEAN CHAMPION
AND I THINK I AM THE SPECIAL ONE."

Josie Mourinho

"I AM THE NORMAL ONE."

Jurgen Klopp

"I DEFINITELY WANT BROOKLYN TO
BE CHRISTENED, BUT I DON'T KNOW
INTO WHAT RELIGION YET."

David Beckham

"WILL CHELSEA QUALIFY WITH EASE? I
THINK SO, BUT IT WON'T BE EASY."

Jamie Redknapp

"IF YOU ARE GOING TO WIN THE
PREMIER LEAGUE, YOU ARE GOING
TO HAVE TO FINISH ABOVE
CHELSEA AND MAN CITY."

Graeme Souness

"ONLY GOD KNOWS WHO WILL GO
THROUGH. YOU'RE TALKING TO HIM."

Zlatan Ibrahimovic

"AT BAYERN WE HAVE ROBERT LEWANGOALSKI..... YOU KNOW.... ROBERT LEWAN...GOALSKI."

Thomas Muller

"I'M MORE AFRAID OF MY MUM THAN SVEN-GÖRAN ERIKSSON OR DAVID MOYES."

Wayne Rooney

"MY WIFE DOESN'T LIKE FOOTBALL. ONE DAY SHE CALLED ME 10 MINUTES BEFORE A GAME TO FIND OUT WHERE I WAS."

Peter Crouch

"THEY'RE LUCKY I DIDN'T COME 10 YEARS AGO BECAUSE I WOULD BE THE PRESIDENT TODAY"

Zlatan Ibrahimovic on the MLS

"I ASKED MY SON WHO HIS FAVOURITE PLAYER WAS. I EXPECTED HIM TO SAY 'YOU, DAD'. BUT HE SAID THIERRY HENRY."

Didier Drogba

"SOMETIMES IN FOOTBALL YOU HAVE TO SCORE GOALS".

Thierry Henry

"FOOTBALL WAS MY ONLY HOPE IN LIFE. I WASN'T TOO GOOD AT SCHOOL. TO GIVE YOU AN IDEA, I MANAGED TO FAIL ART IN A CLASS WHERE MY UNCLE WAS THE TEACHER."

Richarlison

"I HAD NO IDEA WHO MY TEAMMATES AT GENOA WERE WHEN I SIGNED. SO I TURNED ON MY PLAYSTATION AND LOOKED THEM UP ON FIFA."

Krzysztof Piątek

"I SHOULDN'T SAY THIS - DEFINITELY NOT NOW! BUT WHEN I WAS YOUNG I WAS A MASSIVE UNITED FAN"

Raheem Sterling

"WHAT A SHOT! THAT'S COMPLETELY UNSTOPPABLE, BUT THE KEEPER'S GOT TO DO BETTER FOR ME."

Michael Owen

'WINNING DOESN'T REALLY MATTER AS LONG AS YOU WIN'

Vinny Jones

"MY PARENTS HAVE ALWAYS BEEN THERE FOR ME... EVER SINCE I WAS ABOUT SEVEN."

David Beckham

"FOOTBALLERS THESE DAYS OFTEN
HAVE TO USE THEIR FEET."

Michael Owen

"I DON'T WANT ROONEY TO LEAVE
THESE SHORES BUT IF HE DOES, I
THINK HE'LL GO ABROAD."

Ian Wright

"GIROUD SCORED A BRILLIANT
HEADER WITH THE LAST KICK OF
THE GAME."

Chris Kamara

"THAT'S A FANTASTIC PENALTY, BUT HE'LL BE GUTTED IT WENT WIDE."

Michael Owen

"I THINK ONE OF THESE TEAMS COULD WIN THIS."

Andy Townsend

"I COULDN'T SETTLE IN ITALY – IT WAS LIKE LIVING IN A FOREIGN COUNTRY."

Ian Rush

"MESSI SCORES A GOAL AND CELEBRATES. CRISTIANO SCORES A GOAL AND POSES LIKE HE'S IN A SHAMPOO COMMERCIAL."

Diego Maradonna

"I THINK ONE OF THESE TEAMS COULD WIN THIS." ALEX FERGUSON IS THE BEST MANAGER I'VE EVER HAD AT THIS LEVEL. WELL, HE'S THE ONLY MANAGER I'VE ACTUALLY HAD AT THIS LEVEL. BUT HE'S THE BEST MANAGER I'VE EVER HAD."

David Beckham

"WELL, EITHER SIDE COULD WIN IT, OR IT COULD BE A DRAW."

Ron Atkinson

"DESPITE THE RAIN, IT'S STILL RAINING HERE AT OLD TRAFFORD."

Jimmy Hill

"I'LL NEVER PLAY AT WEMBLEY AGAIN, UNLESS I PLAY AT WEMBLEY AGAIN."

Kevin Keegan

"FOOTBALL'S ALL ABOUT 90 MINUTES."

Glenn Hoddle

"I HEARD BAYERN
LOST.........HAHAHAHAHAHA."

Jurgen Klopp

"THERE ARE TWO TYPES OF
MANAGER... THOSE WHO HAVE BEEN
SACKED AND THOSE WHO WILL BE
SACKED IN THE FUTURE"

Terry Venables

"MOST PEOPLE SCORE BETWEEN
THE POSTS"

Jamie Redknapp

THE ULTIMATE
FOOTBALL
FACTS

WHILE ZLATAN IBRAHIMOVIC YOUTH
TEAM WERE 4-0 DOWN, ZLATAN
CAME ON AS A SUBSTITUTE AND
SCORED 8 GOALS!

CRISTIANO RONALDO WAS NAMED
AFTER FORMER US PRESIDENT
RONALD REGAN.

STEVEN GERRARD HAS SWAPPED
HIS SHIRT WITH OVER 100 PLAYERS,
BUT NEVER WITH A MAN UNITED
PLAYER!

RONALDINHO FIRST GAINED MEDIA
ATTENTION WHEN HIS YOUTH
TEAM 23-0. HE SCORED ALL 23
GOALS!

HARRY KANE WAS REJECTED BY
ARSENAL WHEN HE WAS 11 BECAUSE
HE WAS A 'LITTLE CHUBBY'.

THE DIFFERENCE BETWEEN MESSI'S
AGE AND RONALDO'S AGE IS 869
DAYS, THE SAME DIFFERENCE
BETWEEN RONALDO'S SON AND
MESSI'S SON!

THE MOST AMOUNT OF GOALS SCORED
IN ONE GAME WAS BACK IN DECEMBER
OF 1942, STEPHAN STANIS SCORED A
STAGGERING 16 GOALS FOR HIS CLUB
RACING CLUB DE LENS, A RECORD WHICH
STILL STANDS TO THIS DAY.

THE FASTEST GOAL SCORED WAS
BY ARGENTINE RICARDO OLIVERA,
WHICH CLOCKED 2.8 SECONDS FROM
KICK OFF!

NAC BREDA IS THE CLUB WITH THE
LONGEST NAME IN THE WORLD,
WHICH STANDS FOR NOOIT OPGEVEN
ALTIJD DOORZETTEN AANGENAAM
DOOR VERMAAK EN NUTTIG DOOR
ONTSPANNING COMBINATIE BREDA.

BRAZIL HOLD THE RECORD FOR THE
MOST NUMBER OF WORLD CUP
WINS, 5. THEY HAVE ALSO REACHED
THE FINALS 7 TIMES, 1 LESS THAN
GERMANY WHO HOLD THE RECORD
FOR MOST WORLD CUP FINALS..

USA AND CANADA ARE THE ONLY
COUNTRIES IN THE WORLD THAT
CALL FOOTBALL SOCCER!

THE FIRST EVER INTERNATIONAL
FOOTBALL MATCH WAS ON 30TH
OF NOVEMBER 1872, BETWEEN
ENGLAND AND SCOTLAND. THE
MATCH ENDED 0-0.

MARK HUGHES IS THE ONLY
PROFFESIONAL FOOTBALLER WHO
PLAYED FOR TWO CLUBS ON THE
SAME DAY – BAYERN MUNICH AND
WALES!

THE NAME "SOCCER" WAS ACTUALLY
CREATED BY THE ENGLISH, BUT
DECIDED TO STOP USING IT MORE
THAN 35 YEARS AGO!

THE HIGHEST-SCORING GAME CAME AT 2002 WHEN A S ADEMA WON 149- 0 AGAINST SO L'EMYRNE. SO L'EMYRNE DECIDED TO PROTEST DUE TO AN UNFAIR REFEREE DECISION IN THE PREVIOUS GAME. THIS RESULTED IN THE TEAM SCORING 149 OWN GOALS!

THE OLDEST FOOTBALL PLAYER IS KAZUYOSHI MIURA WHO IS 53 YEARS OLD! HE CURRENTLY PLAYS FOR JAPANESE CLUB YOKOHOMA FC.

THE MOST GOALS SCORED BY ANY
GOALKEEPER IS BY BRAZIALIAN
ROGERIO CENI FOR SAO PAULO FC,
WHICH TALLIES UP TO 131 CAREER
GOALS! ANY STRIKER WOULD BE
PROUD OF THAT NUMBER.

THE LONGEST EVER UNBEATEN
STREAK IS HELD BY ROMANIAN
SIDE STEAUA BUCHAREST, WHO
WENT 106 MATCHES UNBEATEN
AND WON STRAIGHT LEAGUE TITLES
ALONG WITH THE 1985-86
EUROPEAN CUP.

THE MOST RED CARDS EVER PRODUCED
IN ONE MATCH WAS IN THE 5TH TIER
ARGENTINEAN FOOTBALL LEAGUE, ARCH-
RIVALS CLAYPOLE AND VICTORIANO
ARENAS. A TOTAL OF 36 RED CARDS WAS
PRODUCED TO ALL PLAYERS, INCLUDING
ALL THE COACHES AND SUBSTITUES!

CRISTIANO RONALDO HAS SCORED A
GOAL FOR EVERY MINUTE OF A
FOOTBALL GAME. HE HAS SCORED
MOST FREQUENTLY IN THE 23RD
MINUTE OF GAMES.

PELE WON THE WORLD CUP IN 1958 AT
ONLY 17 YEARS OLD. HE SCORED 6 GOALS,
IN THAT TOURNAMENT, HE ALSO IS THE
ONLY PLAYER TO WIN THREE WORLD
CUPS (1958, 1962 AND 1970).

THE FIRST EVER GAME OF
BASKETBALL WAS ACTUALLY
PLAYED WITH A FOOTBALL!

NEIL ARMSTRONG (THE FIRST MAN ON THE MOON) WANTED TO TAKE A FOOTBALL TO THE MOON WITH HIM BUT NASA DIDN'T ALLOW IT BECAUSE THEY THOUGHT IT WAS UN-AMERICAN.

REAL MADRID HAS WON THE MOST CHAMPIONS LEAGUE FINALS AT A WHOPPING 13!

AT AGE 13 KYLIAN MBAPPE HAD
TRIALS AT CHELSEA, BUT WAS
REJECTED BECAUSE HE WAS TOO
BAD AT DEFENDING.

GERMAN GOALKEEPER TOM STARKE
PLAYED FOR BAYERN MUNICH FOR 6
YEARS AND ONLY PLAYED 12 GAMES.
WITHIN THAT TIME HE WON 15
TROPHIES, INCLUDING 1 CHAMPIONS
LEAGUE AND 5 BUNDESLIGA MEDALS.
TO PUT IT INTO PERSPECTIVE, THAT
IS MORE THAN A MEDAL PER GAME!

SOUTH KOREAN JUNG-HWAN AHN
SCORED THE WINNING GOAL IN THE
2-1 VICTORY OVER ITALY IN THE 2002
WORLD CUP. AFTERWARDS, HIS
ITALIAN CLUB, PERUGIA, RELEASED HIM,
STATING AFTERWARDS THAT HE HAD
RUINED ITALIAN FOOTBALL!

ARGENTINE FOOTBALLER ALFREDO
DI STÉFANO PLAYED FOR THREE
DIFFERENT NATIONS DURING HIS
CAREER – ARGENTINA, COLUMBIA.
AND SPAIN.

ERLING HAALAND'S FATHER WAS A
PROFESSIONAL FOOTBALLER, ALF INGE
HAALAND, WHO PLAYED FOR MAN
CITY, BEFORE ROY KEANE
DELIBERATELY INJURED HIM WHICH
CAUSED HIM TO RETIRE.

CRISTIANO RONALDO'S NICKNAME
AS A BABY WAS 'CRYBABY' AS HE
WOULD BURST INTO TEARS
WHENEVER SOMETHING DIDN'T GO
HIS WAY.

ERLING HAALAND MADE A RAP VIDEO
WITH HIS FRIENDS IN 2016, HE CALLED
HIMSELF 'FLOW KINGZ'.

ANTOINE GRIEZMANN VOICED
SUPERMAN FOR THE FRENCH LEGO
BATMAN MOVIE.

INDIA ONCE QUALIFIED FOR THE 1950
WORLD CUP BUT REFUSED TO PLAY
BECAUSE FIFA WOULDN'T LET THEM
PLAY BAREFOOT.

MANUEL NEUER DID THE VOICEOVER
FOR FRANK MCCAY IN THE
GERMAN VERSION OF "MONSTERS
INC."

IN 1996, A MAN CALLED 'ALI DIA' PRETENDED TO BE LEGENDARY FOOTBALLER GEORGE WEAH'S COUSIN AND FAKED HIS WAY INTO GETTING TRIALS AT SOUTHAMPTON. DUE TO INJURIES AT THE CLUB, GRAEME SOUNESS GAVE HIM A ONE MONTH CONTRACT. HE CAME ON AS A SUB AGAINST LEEDS AND WAS LET GO IMMEDIATELY AFTER. HE IS NAMED NUMBER 1 OF "THE 50 WORST FOOTBALLERS" IN THE TIME NEWSPAPER.

GARY NEVILLE'S FATHER IS CALLED NEVILLE NEVILLE

BRAZIL'S FIRST EVER OFFICIAL MATCH
WAS AGAINST EXETER CITY IN 1914.

THE FIRST BRITISH FOOTBALL CLUB
TO REACH A EUROPEAN CHAMPIONS
CUP SEMI-FINAL WAS HIBERNIAN
OF SCOTLAND IN SEASON 1955-56.

STEFAN SCHWARZ HAD AN
INTERESTING CLAUSE IN HIS
CONTRACT WHEN HE SIGNED FOR
SUNDERLAND IN 1999: HE WAS
BANNED FROM TRAVELING INTO
SPACE!

REAL MADRID ONCE BEAT THEIR B
TEAM 6-1 IN THE 1980 COPA DEL
REY FINAL.

WHEN MARIO BALOTELLI WON BIG AT A CASINO IN MANCHESTER, HE SPOTTED A HOMELESS MAN ON THE STREET AND GAVE HIM THOUSANDS OF POUNDS OF HIS OWN MONEY.

DUNDEE UNITED HAVE A 100% RECORD AGAINST BARCELONA. THE SCOTTISH SIDE HAS WON ALL FOUR GAMES AGAINST THE CATALAN GIANTS.

IN THE ANDOVER AND DISTRICT
SUNDAY LEAGUE, REFEREE MARTIN
SYLVESTER SENT HIMSELF OFF
AFTER PUNCHING A PLAYER DURING
A GAME.

THE FIRST TRANSFER WAS IN 1893
FOR JUST OVER £100. WILLIE
GROVES MADE THE SWITCH FROM
WEST BROMWICH ALBION TO
ASTON VILLA.

IN 2010, SPAIN WON THE WORLD CUP, ONLY SCORING 8 GOALS IN THE WHOLE TOURNAMENT!

STEVE BRUCE SCORED 19 GOALS IN ONE SEASON AS A CENTRE-BACK FOR MANCHESTER UNITED IN 1990-91.

WHY NOT LEAVE A REVIEW?

YOU CAN LEAVE. REVIEW AT:

AMAZON.CO.UK/REVIEW/CREATE-REVIEW?ASIN=B0934LRCYG&

OR SCAN BELOW TO TAKE YOU TO THE REVIEW PAGE

THANK YOU AND KEEP BALLIN'!

Made in the USA
Monee, IL
05 December 2024

72652088R00059